W9-AEX-621

P. Hermit
Claims a Castle

written by **Marcia Trimble**   illustrated by **George Ulrich**

Images Press – Los Altos Hills, California

Published by Images Press

No part of this publication may be reproduced, or stored in a retrieval system, or transmitted in any form or by any means, electronic, mechanical, photocopying, recording, or otherwise, without permission of the publisher.
For information regarding permission write to Images Press, 27920 Roble Alto Street, Los Altos Hills, California 94022

Publisher's Cataloging-in-Publication
(Provided by Quality Books, Inc.)

Trimble, Marcia.
     P. Hermit claims a castle / by Marcia Trimble ; illustrated by George Ulrich. -- 1st ed.
     p. cm.
     SUMMARY: After P. Hermit Crab is taken from his tidepool, he manages to find his way back to his natural habitat, where he can shed his outgrown shell and move into a new one that feels like a castle.
     Preassigned LCCN: 98-94130
     ISBN: 1-891577-44-1 (hbk.)
     ISBN: 1-891577-46-8 (pbk.)

     1. Hermit crabs--Juvenile fiction. 2. Tide pool ecology--Juvenile fiction.
     3. Shells--Juvenile fiction. I. Ulrich, George, ill. II. Title.

PZ7.T734Ph 1999 [E]
QBI98-1589

10 9 8 7 6 5 4 3 2 1

Text was set in Frankfurter and Avant Garde
Book design by MontiGraphics

Printed in Hong Kong by South China Printing Co. (1988) Ltd. on acid free paper. ∞

To all the children who return hermit crabs to the tidepool before leaving the beach.   M.T.

For Leora and Josh   G.U.

"Is that an empty turban...

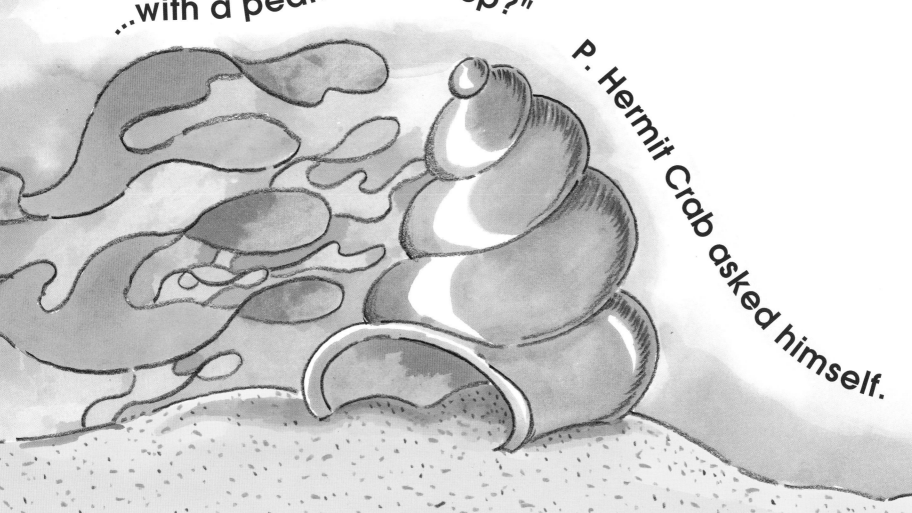

"...with a pearl on the top?" P. Hermit Crab asked himself.

He crawled closer to inspect the silver turban...when...

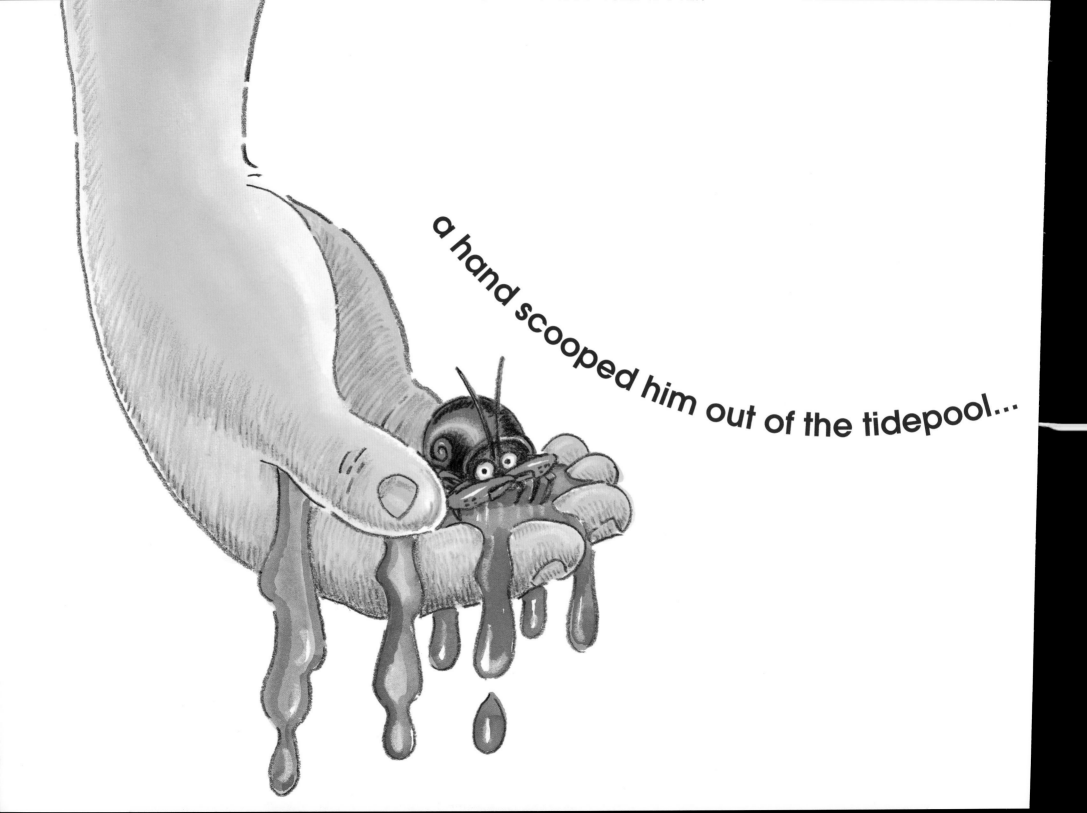

a hand scooped him out of the tidepool...

and
dropped
him
into
a
sandpail.

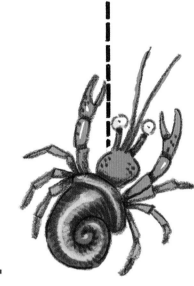

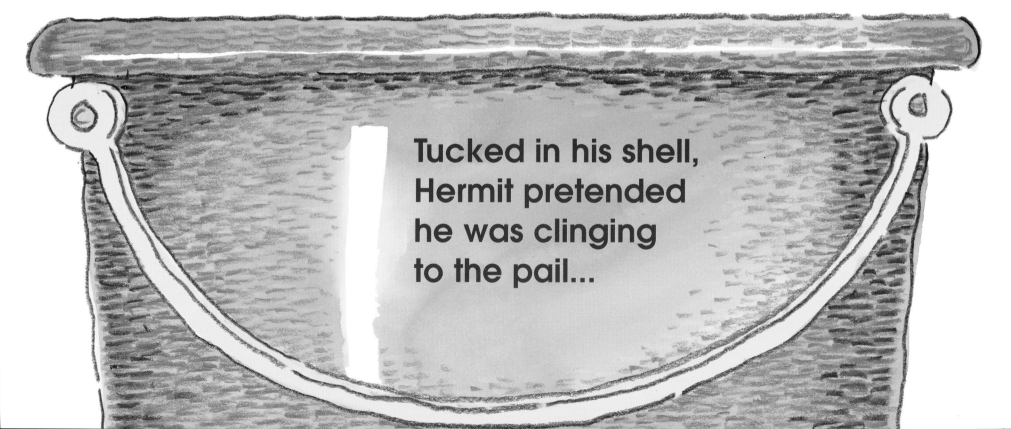

Tucked in his shell,
Hermit pretended
he was clinging
to the pail...

but when Peter Paget was not looking...

Hermit crawled up the side...

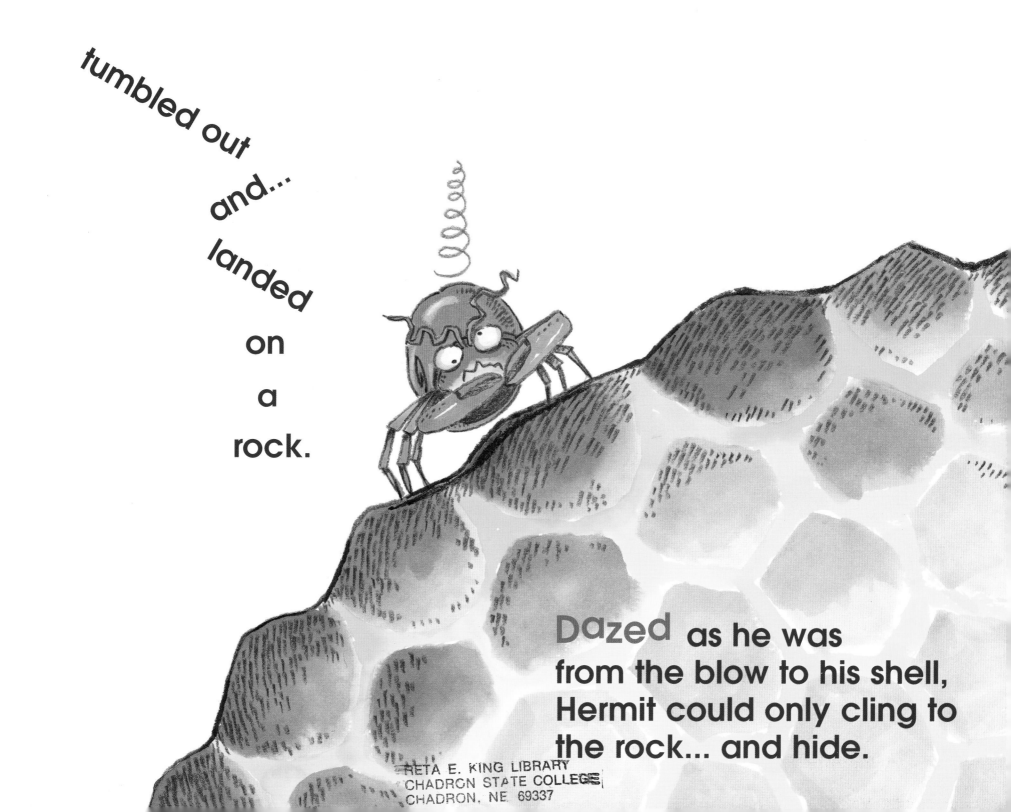

tumbled out
and...
landed
on
a
rock.

Dazed as he was
from the blow to his shell,
Hermit could only cling to
the rock... and hide.

Stars
shimmered
before his eyes.
A vision
of colors and patterns
dazzled
his senses...
a kaleidoscope
of
olive
and
gold
streaks,
red edges
and
yellow spots,
a web
of
yellow lines and stripes,
scrolls...
and
speckles...
and
ridges.

Hermit grinned a starry-eyed grin.

"I have landed
in a sea of shells...

shells fit for a prince.

I will claim a shell
for my kingdom
in the sea,"
he declared to himself.

"I will claim this olive shell with gold outlines
and a thick wall. But for what end?"
Prince Hermit asked himself.
"Ah! For my castle, of course!"

"I beg your pardon.
This shell is occupied,"
said a leopard tortoise.
"I am looking for dry rough ground
for my stumpy legs to walk on."

The tortoise showed the Prince that he could withdraw his head and legs and tail into his shell.

"What a showoff!" said the Prince.
"You can hide inside your suit of armor
but you will always have to carry
the same shell on your back.

One shell is not enough for me."

"I will claim this shell
with red edges
for my castle,"
exclaimed the Prince.

"I beg your pardon,"
said a painted turtle.
"This shell is occupied.
I have walked and walked
and I am on my way
to a fresh water pond
to use my webbed feet
for swimming."

"You can walk and swim
all you want and show off
your suit of armor, too.
But you will always carry
the same shell on your back.

One shell is not enough for me."

"I will claim this shell
with a yellow and orange turret
for my castle."

"I beg your pardon,"
said a box turtle.
**"This high dome is
occupied.**
I am on my way to the woods.
Come and eat
strawberries with me."

"Thank you, but I do not
eat strawberries...
you will always eat
strawberries and show off
your suit of armor, too.
But you will always carry
the same shell
on your back.

One shell is not enough for me."

"I will claim this round flat shell
with bumps and spots
for my castle."

"I beg your pardon,"
said the soft-shelled turtle
with a shell of leathery skin.
"This shell is occupied.
I hide in the mud and sand
and use my long nose
for a breathing tube,"
he boasted.

"I cannot build a castle
in the sand...
or live in the same shell,"
said the Prince.

"One shell is not enough for me."

Only one shell left.
"This shell will have to do for my castle."

"**I beg your pardon,**"
said an African pancake tortoise.
"**This shell is occupied.**
I am looking for a crack
in a rock to wedge into."

"How do you wedge into a crack?"
asked the Prince.
"I have a flat flexible shell.
I take a deep breath and inflate my body,
and then I can wedge tightly
into the crack."
"I prefer to find safety in my castle,"
said the Prince.
"Besides, you will always carry
the same shell on your back.

One shell is not enough for me."

The turtles are wrapped up
in their shells,
thought the Prince.

He crawled to the sand.

Sunlight streaked through
the ripples on the water.
"Is that a shell drifting out of the sea?"
Hermit asked himself.
"It is moving too fast
to be unoccupied.
It must be the green sea turtle.
I guess it's because
he can't withdraw into his shell
that he has to play so hard to get."
And before Hermit could call out
for a ride to the ocean
the green sea turtle raced away
using his paddlelike flippers.
"He will always carry
the same shell on his back,"
said Hermit.

"One shell is not enough for me."

The sun was setting.
The colors and patterns
were fading
into dark shadows.
I have been building air castles,
thought Hermit Crab.
I must find a silver turban
with a pearl on the top.

A turtle was just digging
its way out of a hole
in the sand.
Hermit crawled upon
the newborn turtle.
"Will you take me
to my tidepool?"
he asked.
The hatchling said,
"Come along with me,
I am going to the sea.
I must crawl to the water
before the birds and mammals
flock to the beach to eat me.
I must swim while it is dark
so the birds will not swoop
into the water and attack me."

A wave washed over the baby turtle... and tossed Hermit into the sea.

Hermit wasn't imagining it...

he was **surfing** a wave.

The wave washed him into a tidepool... and linked him back in the foodchain.

Hermit looked at a sea snail. If he chose the sea snail, he might latch onto a feast.

He looked at a seashell.
He could choose from
all the seashells
in the tidepool
after high tide.

"Ah! Is that an empty turban...

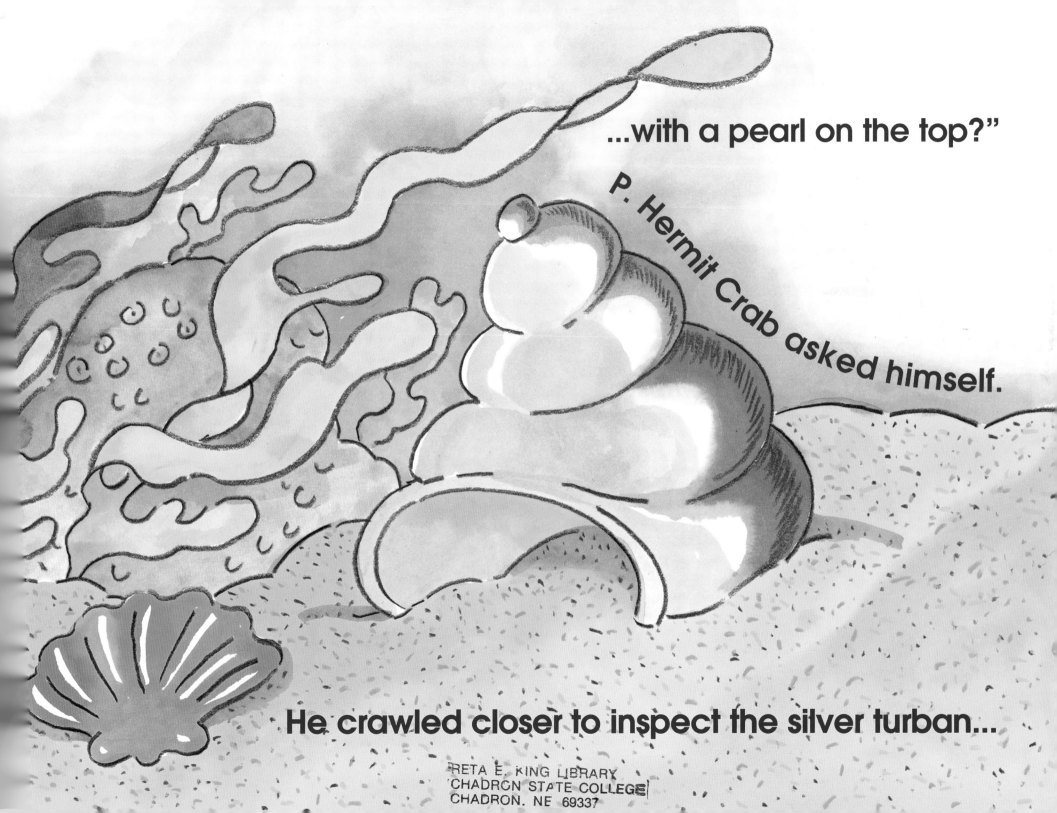

"...with a pearl on the top?"

P. Hermit Crab asked himself.

He crawled closer to inspect the silver turban...

twisted out of his old shell...

backed up
the spiral staircase
of the empty turret...

and raised
the drawbridge
with his claws.

This shell fits just right.
A castle fit for a prince,
he thought.
For now
this is the home for me...

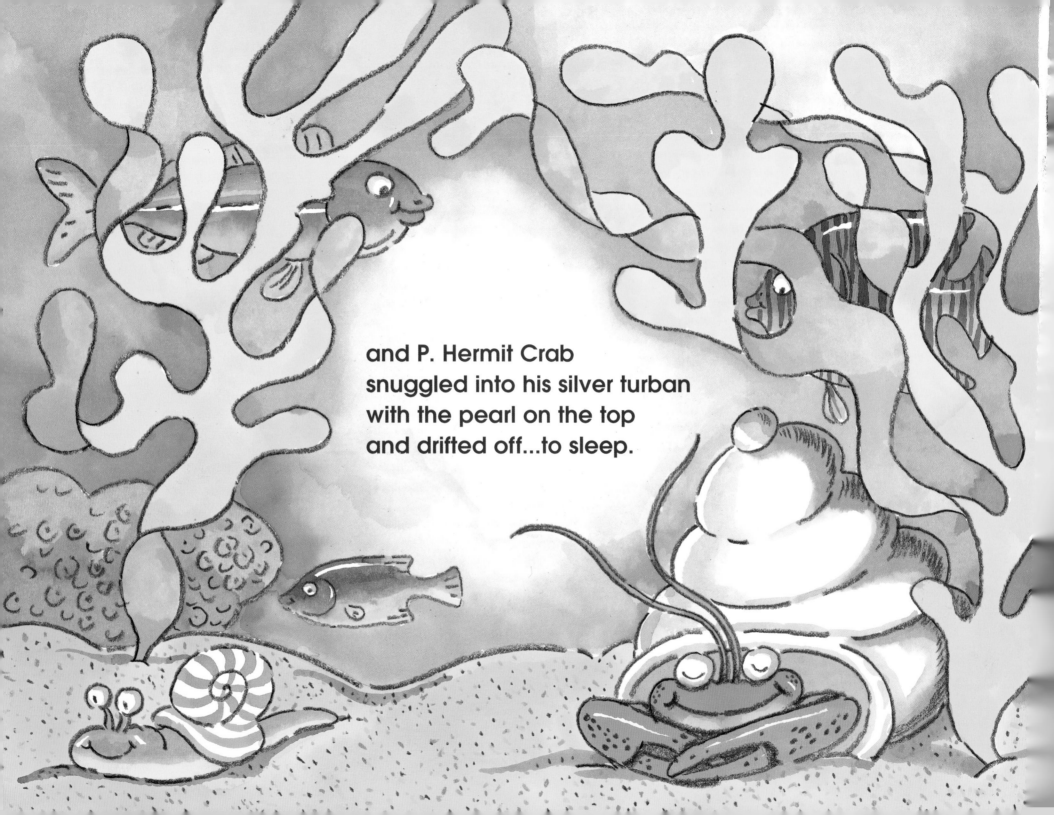

and P. Hermit Crab
snuggled into his silver turban
with the pearl on the top
and drifted off...to sleep.